MEMILY

Written by Stephen Cosgrove
Illustrated by Robin James

A Serendipity™ Book

PRICE STERN SLOAN
Los Angeles

The Serendipity Series was created by Stephen Cosgrove and Robin James.

A miniature edition of this title in a
Serendipity Mini Book and Plush Toy Set was published in 1994.

Copyright © 1995, 1994, 1987 Price Stern Sloan, Inc.
Published by Price Stern Sloan, Inc.,
A member of The Putnam & Grosset Group, New York, New York.

ISBN 0-8431-3822-X

Serendipity˜ and The Pink Dragon® are trademarks of Price Stern Sloan, Inc.

First Revised Edition
1 3 5 7 9 10 8 6 4 2

Library of Congress Cataloging-in-Publication Data
Cosgrove, Stephen.
Memily / written by Stephen Cosgrove; illustrated by Robin James.
p. cm.
"Serendipity"—T.p. verso
Summary: The other jungle animals make Memily the giraffe self-conscious about her size, until
a meeting with another giraffe convinces her that she is just right for the kind of animal she is.
ISBN 0-8431-3822-X
[1. Giraffes—Fiction. 2. Jungle animals—Fiction. 3. Self-acceptance—Fiction.
4. Size—Fiction.] I. Title.
PZ7.C8187Me 1995
[E]—dc20   94-25728
                                                                  CIP
                                                                  AC

Dedicated to the one and only Emily,
pronounced Memily . . . one of a kind in a
land of duplication.

—*Stephen*

There was a land; a marvelous, green, sweet-smelling land called the Jasmine Jungle. A land brimming with all the mystery of life and filled with the raucous sounds of all the creatures who lived within. It was here that baby leopards leaped. It was here that elephants of all sizes spritzed and sprayed the jungle with a fine watery mist, causing rainbows to dance from sunbeam to sunbeam. This was the magical Jasmine Jungle.

In the middle of this land was a meadow. And in this fragrant meadow a small knobby-kneed giraffe named Memily was born. Normally, this would not have been such a special event, but until Memily was born there were only two other giraffes in the jungle: Memily's father and, of course, Memily's mother. All the other creatures of the jungle gathered around and "oohhed" and "ahhed" at the newborn baby.

Memily spent the first few weeks of life in the Jasmine Jungle awkwardly learning how to walk. As we all know, giraffes have long, lanky legs, and Memily was no exception. It took her a long time to learn to walk on legs that were so long. She would wobble about the meadow bouncing off a tree here and a bush there as she struggled to gain her balance.

Memily had a problem of sorts. She knew that she was a giraffe, there was no problem with that. She knew about all the dangers of the jungle, for her mother had taught her well. Memily's problem was that she didn't have anybody to play with who was her own size.

One day she joined a bunch of bunnies in playing a silly forest game. She thought to herself, What fun! I just love to play tag. Soon a bunny tagged her "it," and she was off chasing the little creatures all over the meadow.

Memily felt just like a bunny—only a lot taller.

The game started innocently, then ended
in disaster. One minute, Memily was chasing
the bunnies, and the next minute she tripped
on a root that the others had jumped over.
She flipped; she flopped; and landed in a heap
right on top of all the little bunnies.

One by one, the bunnies popped to their feet out of this jungle jumble, until the only one left in the pile of confusion was Memily.

"Gee whiz, Memily!" the bunnies cried. "You could have hurt us that way! You have got to play with someone your own size!"

With that, the bunnies hopped away, leaving Memily tangled and confused in the middle of the path. Well, she thought, I'll just have to find someone taller to play with.

She struggled to her feet and galloped clumsily on her way, in search of new friends and new games.

Now Memily's only problem with finding someone her own size was the fact that Memily was still growing. Day by day she grew taller and taller. She tried to play with the lions, but they were too short and much too rough. She tried to play with the monkeys, but Memily had trouble walking on the ground, let alone climbing the trees.

Finally, Memily befriended two zebras and an elephant who were playing a rousing game of hide-and-go-seek. They had no objections to letting Memily play. For, as you know, the more the merrier when you are playing hide-and-go-seek.

One of the zebras counted to ten while the others hid. The elephant hid in the river, with only his trunk sticking out like a reed. The other zebra hid in the bush where her stripes disguised her.

Memily dashed this way and that looking for somewhere to hide. She tried to hide in the water with the elephant, but she was much too tall, and besides, she didn't have a trunk to breathe through. She tried to hide in the bush with the zebra, but her neck stuck way out like a weed in the willows.

Finally, she found a place to hide—or at least she thought she was hiding. But when the other zebra finished counting to ten he instantly spied Memily behind a pile of rocks in the clearing. Just where could a very tall giraffe hide?

She hid here. She hid there. But her gangly legs or her long neck always stuck out.

Finally, the zebras and the elephant said, "It's just not going to work, Memily! You are just too tall. You have to find someone your own size. Maybe you should just play with the trees." Giggling, the three of them dashed deep into the Jasmine Jungle, leaving Memily all alone with no one to play with.

She searched high and low for someone her own size, but she could find no one. Finally, resolved that there was no one as tall as she was, Memily stopped trying to play games with any of the other creatures of the forest.

Week after week Memily grew, and she became sadder and sadder. She was shy and embarrassed by her height, and whenever any of the other creatures walked by she would turn her head, knowing that they had to look up just to look her in the eye.

Memily grew and grew. She began to bow her neck and bend her knees, trying to make herself shorter. Everything she tried was to no avail, for no matter how much she bowed her neck or bent her knees, she was still very tall indeed.

Memily was so embarrassed about being tall that she began spending all of her days hiding amidst the trees that grew at the edge of the Jasmine Jungle. She would stand for hours, munching on sweet leaves and twitching her ears so that the birds wouldn't build a nest on her head.

But the birds would come anyway, twittering and giggling and, while standing on Memily's head, they would bend over, look her in the eye and sing a silly song:

> "Who can you see . . .
> Taller than a tree?
> It's Memily!
> It's Memily!"

Memily would shake her head and the birds would flutter away laughing.

One day, as Memily was rustling through the uppermost branches of a very tall tree, she was shocked nearly out of her wits by the appearance of another head looking back at her from another tree. She looked once, she looked twice, and sure enough there was another giraffe just as tall as she.

"Hello, there," she said shyly. "Do you have to hide in the trees, too?"

The other giraffe laughed and laughed, and walked over to Memily's tree in a graceful, swaying motion. "No!" he said in a gentle rumble. "I am not hiding in the tree. I am eating the sweet leaves that only grow at the very top. My name is Herschel. Who are you?"

"Memily," she said as she stepped from behind the tree with her knees bent and her neck bowed.

Herschel laughed as Memily walked in her awkward way. "Why are you walking like that?"

"I have to walk this way," said Memily shyly. "Otherwise I would be much taller than the other creatures!"

"But you are supposed to be taller than the other creatures," said Herschel. "It is the way of nature. Some creatures are tall, some are small, but all have their place in the Jasmine Jungle."

With the passage of time, Herschel taught Memily that being tall is not bad and that in nature all creatures are special in their own way.

SHORT IS SHORT

AND TALL IS TALL.

YOU ARE WHAT YOU ARE,

AND THAT IS ALL!

Serendipity™ Books

Created by
Stephen Cosgrove and Robin James

Enjoy all the delightful books in the Serendipity™ Series:

Also look for our Serendipity™ Mini Book and Plush Toy Sets:

The above books, and many others, can be bought wherever books are sold.

PRICE STERN SLOAN
Los Angeles